Saddled With Desire

An Interracial Monster Romance

Blaise Monroe

Copyright © 2023 by Blaise Monroe

All rights reserved.

This book or any portion thereof may not be reproduced or used in any manner whatsoever without the

express written permission of the publisher, except as permitted by U.S. copyright law.

This is a work of fiction. Any characters, names, places, brands, media and incidents are used solely in a fictitious nature based

on the author's imagination. Any resemblance to or mention of persons, places, organizations or other incidents is purely coincidental.

The author greatly appreciates that you've taken the time to read this work.

Thank you for supporting Blaise Monroe.

Contents

Foreward		V
1.	Chapter 1	1
2.	Chapter 2	10
3.	Chapter 3	19
4.	Chapter 4	24
5.	Chapter 5	34
6.	Chapter 6	44
7.	Chapter 7	52
8.	Chapter 8	61
9.	Chapter 9	66
10.	Chapter 10	71
11.	Chapter 11	79
12.	Chapter 12	86

13. Author's Note 97

Foreward

This standalone novella is perfect for those who not only enjoy but crave thrilling monster romances between captivating ethnic heroines and sexy male shifters. For those who have yet to experience this subject matter, are you ready to be swept away in a riveting monster romance? Then indulge in this dark romance today.

Warning: This book contains mature themes, so the reader's discretion is advised.

Chapter 1

"Please, please don't do this," the man whimpered, his words swallowed by the engulfing darkness of the room. He felt a trickle at his lips; his own blood. "You don't have to do this."

Devyn stepped into the light of the dismal chamber, her presence much larger and more powerful in the expanse space than her five-foot-five height. "Interesting choice of words, Tommy." Her leather gloves glinted menacingly as she perched herself on the wooden chair across from him. She tilted her head slightly, and her stylish box braids, tied back in a neat ponytail, swayed with the action. "Tell me, she began softly, her voice like a soft hush in the night. "Is that what your victim said right before you stole his innocence? Before you snuffed out his life?" she asked, flashing the man a look that sent a chill up his spine.

Tommy blinked rapidly, his mouth opening and closing voicelessly as he searched for a response that would not come to him.

"See, that's the problem with people like you," Devyn continued, ignoring him. "You want the mercy you're unwilling to give others. You know I have eyes and ears all over these streets, yet you still chose to harm a boy for your own amusement. You might think you can do whatever you want. But understand this; *no one escapes their Karma.*"

He felt the weight of her cold gaze like a physical force pressing him against his seat. "I didn't mean to kill him! It was an accident! I don't know my own strength. I'd never hurt him!" he cried out. His voice echoed off the walls of the dingy, cold room, reverberating through his body in time with the beating of his heart.

His plea was met only with a menacing smile, followed by a mirthless laugh. It was a chilling sound, like a thousand icicles dripping from the sky.

She drew nearer to him, her smile slipping instantly, only to be replaced by an intense, grave look. "You repulse me," Devyn spoke quietly. "He may not have been able to survive you, but I will be his justice." She positioned her fingers into the shape of a gun and pointed at him. "Pick a number, one through three."

Tommy let out a pathetic whimper, "Who are you to judge me anyway? To decide my punishment? Only God can do that!"

But Devyn merely exhaled a placid breath in response. She noted inwardly that every time she and her crew apprehended these savage criminals, they suddenly wanted to prattle on about God. They were all the same. "Tommy," she drew out his name like a somber chant to bring his attention back to the situation at hand. "Pick. Your. Number."

"T-two."

Her full, red lips lifted in a genuine smile this time, and Tommy would have thought her beautiful if she wasn't making a game of taking his life.

Devyn whistled. "Two is my personal favorite." Shutting an eye, she aimed at the center of his forehead. "Forgoes both temples and cuts right through the bullshit."

"Don't!"

Devyn gave a ghostly pull of an invisible trigger and a thunderous sound roared through the chamber. Tommy's corpse crumpled to the ground like a discarded ragdoll, his sightless eyes gazing eternally upon Devyn. Thick liquid pooled around him like a rich fabric, as Devyn slowly rose, delicately laying a note on his chest for the authorities. "There's a special place in hell for people like you," she said. "May you think of me often as you all rot together."

Three Days Later

"Detective Grant. Is this a good time?" Devyn asked as she stood in the doorway of the detective's office. The look of surprise on the man's face made her smile inwardly.

He scowled at Devyn, irritated by her mere presence. "What makes you think I planned to pay you a visit?"

Devyn's smirk became a broad grin, and she wore a mask of pure bravado as she deliberately, confidently strode toward his desk. She slammed her hands down on its sleek surface, unflinchingly locking eyes with Grant. "Because we've been doing this dance for two years, Detective. We both know how it goes. Whenever a piece of shit dies in this city, you burst into my office and accuse *me* ... even though you have no evidence."

Grant curtly motioned for Devyn to take a seat and she withdrew from his desk, settling into the chair opposite him. "Tommy Hudson's face has been plastered all over the news since yesterday," the man spoke warily. "Apparently, *someone* blew his brains out ... and let me guess, you know nothing about that?"

"Can't say that I do."

"Then why are you here?"

She glanced at her french tip, coffin nails which complimented her deep rich brown complexion, stunningly. "Damn, I really need a fill-in. Anyway, I plan on having lunch with Trixie in an hour not too far from here, so I figured I could kill two birds with one stone."

Grant arched his eyebrow. "Interesting choice of words, considering the Alvarez brothers were found crushed to death under a boulder last month."

Devyn lifted her shoulder in a shrug. "It's a turn of phrase, Detective, you know that. So let's cut to the chase. I didn't kill Tommy."

He tossed a bag containing a slip of paper her way. "And I bet you know nothing about this as well."

Picking it up, Devyn read it aloud. "There is no veritable monster worse than man. Tommy Hudson, rapist and murderer of Kory Micheals, age sixteen." Devyn tossed the bag back his way. "Sounds to me like he deserved a lot more than a bullet to the head. Whoever did this, probably did you guys a favor. From what I've heard they do to child predators in prison, you would have been scraping him off his cell floor in no time."

"Goddammit Devyn!" Detective Grant shouted, slamming his fist onto the desk. "We were *so* close to getting him on Kory's assault and murder. You didn't need to interfere!"

"Close, huh?" she repeated, doubtfully. "You mean like how you all were *close* to convicting Officer Miller's brother, Rayes?"

"Not all cops are like him, Devyn. Some of us are good, honest people."

"Maybe you should visit my sister's grave and tell her that." She stood. "Like I said, I didn't kill Tommy ... but I won't pretend to feel bad about his passing. Now if you'll excuse me, I have other places to be."

As she walked to the door, Grant called out to her.

"You're not invincible! No matter how much you think you are. I *know* you're responsible for this."

The sound of high heels clicking against tiled floors ceased as Devyn paused midstep. She turned and looked at him over her shoulder, face void of emotion. "Then prove it," she dared him, and slammed the door behind her.

"You really know how to rile that man up," Trixie said, and took a bite of her chicken fajita sandwich. "From what I heard he was so flustered, he spilled coffee all over himself after you left."

Devyn shook her head in amusement. "Not my fault that he makes things harder than they need to be. I told him *I* didn't kill Tommy, and that should have been that," she smirked. "By the way, your aim is getting better. Two months ago, it took you two tries to land a fatal." She touched her hand to her heart, in a most dramatic fashion, and sniffed. "I'm proud of you."

"I can only get better when I'm learning from the best," Trixie replied, winking. "Seriously though," she said, tucking a lock of her blond bob behind her ear, "thank you for this. I know it was a risk, but because of you, Aunt Mary feels like she can finally breathe."

Devyn lifted her skewer and took a bite of her maple-glazed shrimp. "Family looks out for family. You're mine as much as I'm yours. Never forget that."

Trixie's green eyes softened. "Ditto," she agreed. "So, when are you going back to work?"

"Who said I was going back? I could always work in the shop with you."

"No disrespect, Dev, but you can hardly paint your toes. You'd run my shop into the ground if I hired you."

The two shared a laugh, and then Devyn nodded. "Fair enough. I don't know, though. Cyber Security just isn't what it used to be for me anymore. They've been begging me to come back, but I need some more time to sort things out, like you did when you decided not to return to forensics."

Trixie reached for her iced tea, sipping thoughtfully. "That's understandable. It still has its merits, though."

Devyn smiled. "I know that's right." Returning to their meals, Devyn felt a tingle pass through her body. She scoured the patrons of the restaurant and her lips parted when she zeroed in on one. "Who is *that*?" she asked.

"Who's who?"

"Behind you," Devyn whispered, her head lowered so as not to draw attention to herself. "Third table to the left."

Trixie picked up her soup spoon and used its reflection to check out the patron behind her. Spotting a man, she couldn't help but smile. "I have no clue, but he is fine as hell."

Devyn snickered despite herself. "You can really tell through a spoon?"

Trixie deadpanned. "Um, yes. What? You don't think so?"

Devyn played it cool. "He's *alright*. Maybe a little cute, but nothing major."

Trixie saw right through Devyn's act. Amused by her attempts to appear indifferent, Trixie laughed. "Girl, there is 'alright,' 'cute,' and then there is 'fine as hell.' That right there is fine as *hell*."

Devyn couldn't take her eyes off the mysterious stranger. He was so attractive it was almost unreal, as if he'd stepped out of a Greek myth and into the room. Even from where she sat, Devyn could tell if he stood, he would be one of the tallest people in the room. He had olive skin so smooth she wondered if he'd ever suffered a blemish in his life. His wavy, dark hair fell to his well-defined jawline, curling around his ears. His tailored gray suit jacket fit his muscular frame perfectly. And the black-framed glasses he wore finished off the look, adding a sophisticated flair. In short, his fuckable presence stirred something in Devyn. Her heartbeat quickened. Noticing other women ogling him as he sat at his table reading a book, she cut her eyes. "No, seriously, who is he?"

Trixie shrugged. "I honestly don't know. Maybe he just moved here?"

"Nobody moves here without us knowing about it," Devyn reminded her. She didn't like it. A man like that would certainly create a buzz, so why hadn't she heard anything?

"Maybe he — " started Trixie.

"— Shit, he's leaving," Devyn said as she sprang from the table. "I'll be back." Watching the man's movements, she discreetly followed him. As she reached the front door of the restaurant, she looked around, confused. "What the hell?" He was nowhere in sight. She walked outside and glanced from her left to her right. "Where the hell did you go?" she murmured.

"Behind you," a deep voice said, sending prickles up her back. Turning around, she looked up at the beautiful man in front of her. He smiled and tilted his head. "I'm curious. Is this the part where you finally stop staring and greet me properly?"

Chapter 2

"Excuse you?"

The man smiled, eyes bright as he extended a hand to her in greeting. "Name's Cooper, but everyone just calls me 'Coop.' And that was an honest question. When do we move past the staring from a distance phase and properly greet each other?"

Devyn's eyes were focused on his mouth as he spoke each word, noticing that that they were full and perfectly shaped. She wondered what how they felt. Then, her brain finally registered what he'd said.

"I wasn't staring at you!" she protested, feeling the heat rise in her face. Devyn was thankful that her complexion was darker, knowing that if Trixie's skin was her own, her cheeks would be the brightest shade of scarlet.

"Well then, how did you notice that I left?" Coop asked with a mischievous grin. "By the way, I did that because I had hoped you would follow me. I mean, how else would I know you were watching me, unless I was watching *you*, too?"

"Wait, you watching *me*?" Devyn could not hide her rising suspicion. "Why?"

Coop laughed, his perfect teeth on full display. "I thought it would be obvious to someone so perceptive. It's because I think you're gorgeous."

"Please," said Devyn, trying to hide her smile behind a neutral expression. "It's not like I haven't heard that one before."

The gaze he fixed Devyn with left goosebumps on her skin. "I'm sure you have," he agreed easily, "but not from me. Now, before we move onto the next phase of things, I'll need your name." Devyn arched a well-shaped brow and folded her arms. "Are you really going to give me a hard time about your name?" he asked incredulously, mirroring her and folding his arms over his broad chest.

Cute, she thought before sighing. "My name's Devyn."

"Devyn," the man repeated, and Devyn refused to acknowledge how nice her name sounded on his tongue. "Devyn, I know it's sudden, but I'm a man that goes after what he wants. That in mind, I've decided that I'm open to allowing you, to allow *me*, to take you to dinner."

"Sir, I don't even *know* you."

Coop smiled. "Isn't that what dates are for? Hell, if we get along well enough I might consider letting you get to first base." He clutched a set of invisible pearls. "Just don't think less of me after. I'm not usually so brazen, but hey, when you know, you know."

The corners of Devyn's lips lifted in a smile. "You're funny, I'll give you that."

"I'm also cute and mysterious," Coop replied, flashing his best smoldering gaze. "Come on, I know you're curious about me, just like I am about you. Have dinner with me. If we don't click, then at least, this becomes a good story to tell your friends."

"And free food," Devyn added shamelessly.

Coop chuckled at her quip, and Devyn drank in the sound. "And free food," he concurred.

Damn he's fine. Devyn thought as she continued to mull over her decision. It would be a lot easier if there was a dull personality behind his handsome face. But it had taken Coop less than ten minutes to reveal to her that he was probably a lot of things, but dull was not one of them.

Still, the way he'd blown into town without her knowledge left Devyn feeling somewhat cautious. Who *was* he? And, was it really a coincidence that they ended up at the same restaurant?

"Okay," she said. "I'll have dinner with you."

"Great, I'll pick you up at —"

"— and I'll meet you there," she interrupted him. *Like hell I'm giving this total stranger my address.*

"Fine by me," Coop replied, pulling out his phone. He handed it to Devyn, and she typed in her number. "I know the perfect place," Coop continued when she handed his phone back to him. "I'll text you the information and time."

"Alright," Devyn said evenly, as she stubbornly clung to her aloof persona.

The corners of Coop's lips curved up in his heart-stopping smile, and again, Devyn felt her skin tingle. Suddenly, the restaurant doors burst open and Trixie rushed out.

"Devyn!" she called harshly, approaching her swiftly. "I thought you'd left. I was in there mad as hell."

Devyn, surprised, whipped around to face her.

"What in the world have you been doing?" asked Trixie. "Did you find *Mr. Fine-For-No-Reason*?"

"W-what?" Devyn stammered, embarrassed.

Trixie was looking at her like she had two heads. "That hot stranger. Did you find him?"

"Don't you see? He's right — " Turning back around, Devyn's eyes widened. The street was completely empty.

Later

Devyn liked to change up her look, and expressed herself often through her various hairstyles. Tonight, she decided to forgo her braids in exchange for her signature hairstyle

- a cute wash-and-go. Trixie, being the bestie she was, had helped her take them down, which saved Devyn plenty of time to prepare for her date.

"So let me get this straight," said Trixie, watching Devyn lay her edges with precision, as she sat on Devyn's bed. "You went chasing after that sexy mountain of a man..."

Devyn, who stood in front of her dresser, shot her a look of annoyance through the mirror. "His name is *Coop*," she said for the umpteenth time. Presently, Trixie was supposed to be assisting Devyn with her outfit choice but settled on drilling her with questions instead. "And I wasn't *chasing* after him."

Trixie cast her a sly look. "Right. Right. Sorry. So you walked outside — briskly as hell — to track down *Coop*, only to learn that he noticed you staring — er, glancing at him longer than most people glance — because he was staring at you, too. Then he asked you on a date and you agreed? Did I miss anything?"

Devyn turned away from her mirror Trixie to look at the actual Trixie. "Yes, in fact, you did miss something. I agreed to dinner, not a *date*. And that was a *very* complicated way of describing what happened."

Trixie stuck out her tongue playfully and started clicking away at a game on her phone. Devyn walked over to her garment rack where she slipped on a flirty, knee-length red dress that complimented the warm hue of her plum-red lipstick and matching eyeshadow. "That dress says otherwise. It's positively sinful."

"Good. That's the plan," said Devyn, as she put on her favorite white diamond earrings. She finished by spritzing herself with a lavish-smelling perfume. "The more distracted Coop is, the likelier he'll be to trip up and reveal his true intentions."

"You know," said Trixie. "He really could have asked you out because he wants to know who you are."

Donning her heels, Devyn nodded. "I want to know who *Coop* is too. ... If that's even his real name!"

Trixie threw her hands up. "Well, I can see there's no convincing you to have fun. Where did he tell you to meet him?"

"Asterions."

Trixie's eyes almost popped out of her skull. "Damn. Asterions is like celebrity studded. They're booked for months in advance. The only person I know who has a permanent table there is *you*."

"Exactly. So when his little plan to woo me falls through, I can save the day, which will embarrass him and completely throw him further off his game." Devyn grabbed her black faux fur coat and did a spin. "How do I look?"

Trixie looked her up and down. "Babe, you're a damn weapon. "

***

Coop kept glancing at his watch, an unfamiliar nervousness building within him with every moment that passed. Tonight, the street was alive and bustling, with people entering and exiting the surrounding bars. Soft piano melodies from some establishments competed against the pulsing beat of loudspeakers from others. When Coop looked around he saw couples holding hands, and locking lips near the crosswalks. Tearing his attention from the surrounding scene, he rechecked his watch. *She's late,* he thought to himself.

"I'm not late," Devyn said behind him.

Facing her, his lips parted slightly at the red dress that hugged her curves. Her freshly-washed, short hair was a voluminous and healthy halo of curls. The sight of her buttery smooth brown skin tortured him, and the hints of a tattoo on her back and her thigh, were enough to intrigue him. The playful smirk on her full lips pulled him in, and the look on her face as his eyes roamed over her, made him want to forget dinner altogether.

"Devyn," Coop breathed. "You look beautiful." He extended his hand to her, and she moved closer.

"Thank you," she said, taking his hand. "You're not so bad yourself."

Opening the door, Coop escorted Devyn inside the restaurant. He guided her past the long queue of people who stood in line, hoping to merely catch a glimpse of the Asterions' dining room. "There are a lot more people here tonight than I was expecting," he said. "It's almost impossible to get to the hostess."

Devyn regarded him with a sympathetic gaze. "That's Asterions for you. Honestly, I was surprised you wanted to take me here. It's not unusual to have to reserve a seat half a year in advance."

Coop gave her hand a reassuring squeeze before he strode up to the lectern where a hostess was standing. "Pardon me," he said.

"Sorry, we're booked for the next six months," the hostess replied, not looking up from the papers in front of her. "You can leave your name and number and we will reach out to you when something is available."

I knew it. Devyn thought. She muffled her laugh at the fluster on Coop's face when he briefly glanced at her. *Alright, let me put him out of his misery.*

Before she could interject, the hostess raised her head and turned as white as a sheet. "I am so sorry, Mr. Valentin! I almost didn't recognize you. Please forgive me. It will never happen again. Tonight has been a trainwreck, but that is no excuse!" Tears welled in the corners of the woman's eyes.

Coop gave her a warm smile. "Hey, no worries. *Breathe.* It is a madhouse here and I can tell you're working hard. It's alright."

"S-so I won't get written up for this?"

"Not if I can help it. I heard the owners can be jerks, but I'm sure I can talk some sense into them."

She chuckled. "Thank you, and for the record, I've only ever heard nice things about them both," she said, sheepishly.

Devyn watched as the young woman practically fell over herself in Coop's presence. Her hands shook as she grabbed the menus. "You can follow me t-this way Mr. Valentin and —" For the second time of the night she turned three shades lighter than her natural hue. "Ms. Lane. I apologize as well. I meant no harm." It was clear she was talking about more than just the table mishap.

Devyn smiled. "I get it. No harm, no foul," she said, winking. The woman gave her a brief smile, and quickly escorted them to a secluded table near the large glass waterfall.

"Impressive," Devyn said to Coop after the hostess left, and they were seated.

"I could say the same for you," said Coop, eyes roaming over the menu. "From the look on her face, you're a big deal around here."

"Something like that," she replied dismissively. "Now, will you tell me how you're so well known at Asterions?"

Coop leaned forward, looking over his glasses at her, eyes gleaming in amusement. Devyn's breath caught in her throat, knowing she had his full attention. "And again, I thought it would be obvious to someone so perceptive that I own this fine establishment."

Chapter 3

It took Devyn a moment to snap out of her stupor and find her voice. "Actually, I happen to know that the owner of this 'fine establishment' is Vinny Salvador."

"And I own Vinny Salvador," Coop said simply.

Devyn's face hardened, and Coop laughed. "Goodness, I'm only joking. Vinny and I own this place together. We're pretty good friends. Why do you think she said 'owners?'"

"Why hasn't Vinny ever mentioned being a co-owner?" Devyn interrogated him, not willing to just take his word for it.

"Ah, that blame falls on me," the man before her said rather sheepishly, adjusting his glasses. "I've always much preferred being more of a silent partner. I don't like the spotlight, but with Vinny on a six-month hiatus, I had to show my face. I'm here to oversee things in his absence."

Devyn was looking at him with a hint of skepticism etched in her features.

Coop grabbed her hand from across the table. "I want you to do me a favor. Is it possible for you to hang up your detective hat for tonight? I want to get to know you, but I feel like I'm in an interrogation room more than I'm on a date."

Date?! He thinks this is a date? Shit. Get it together, Devyn. Unfortunately, detective work came naturally to her, even to her disadvantage. If she was going to find out anything, Devyn knew she needed them both to lower their guards.

She sighed. "Sorry, Coop. You're right. I will admit, I'm not the best at dating."

Coop leaned back in his chair, and the conversation paused as the wine was served. "And why is that?" he asked after a moment, nodding at the waitress as she lowered their wine glasses onto the table.

"Because other things have always come first," Devyn said simply, picking up her wine glass and swirling it, before sampling its contents.

"Like what?" asked Coop, taking a sip of his wine as well.

"Like taking care of those who can't take care of themselves. Living here for as long as I have, I've met a lot of good people, but I've also met my share of bad ones. I may not be able to help everyone, but I try my best."

Coop eyed her over the rim of his glass. "And how do you do that?"

She smirked. "Now *who's* interrogating *who*?"

Coop put down his wine glass and raised his hands defensively. "Fair enough. No more shop talk for the evening. Agreed?"

"Agreed."

Dinner turned out to be a pleasant surprise. The meals were delicious, and well-portioned. Their conversation flowed easily and several times, they drew the attention of other diners with their unintentionally loud laughter. Devyn shared a few things about herself and learned that, in addition to being successful and intelligent, Coop was upbeat, patient and a great listener. Before Devyn knew it, the restaurant had cleared, and though the staff refused to say anything, it was clear they were exhausted.

"Jesus, I didn't realize it was so late," she said looking around the room at the mostly empty tables.

Coop glanced at his watch. "Neither did I. Let's get out of here and get you to your car."

Exiting the busy restaurant, they were engulfed by the serene night. A chill wind weaved through the comforting darkness, rustling the leaves on nearby trees. Devyn turned to Coop and smiled, her face illuminated by the streetlamp above as she admitted with a genuine smile, "I had fun tonight."

"Me too," the enigmatic man agreed. "Thank you for accompanying me. It's been a while since I've spent time with someone who wanted nothing in return."

"Who said I didn't want anything?" Coop raised his eyebrow, and she pointed. "My car is the opposite way. Think you could give me a ride?"

His smile returned. "That I will happily do." They walked down to a clean and well-maintained, unassuming car. Devyn smiled on the inside as she thought about his statement earlier. As much as she didn't want to admit it, there was something about Coop that not only intrigued her but seemed to set fire to her entire body.

He opened her car door and she slid in. He started the engine and Devyn marveled at his grace - even the way he drove seemed illicitly sexy. Before she knew it, they had arrived at her car. He turned to face her. "You're staring again, Devyn."

"H-huh?" she stammered, then glared. "No. I was not."

"And we find ourselves doing this dance again," he said, unbuckling his seatbelt. "Do you think we can skip the part where you lie this time, though?"

She rolled her eyes. "*There* it is!" she said suddenly. "I was waiting for whatever red flag you have to finally emerge and piss me off. You're such an arrogant —" her words came to a slamming halt when Coop grabbed her in his arms. He clasped her face and looked her deeply in the eyes.

"You knew that the moment you met me — and you like it. Just like I like how fiery you are," he said huskily. He caressed from her face to her neck, and she shivered despite herself. "I can see it every time you look at me. You hate that

I challenge you, but you like that every challenge has action behind it." He leaned forward and kissed the sensitive spot on the back of her ear. Hearing her stifle a moan, he locked eyes with her once more. "It's up to you how you want tonight to end. We can say goodnight and go our separate ways, or..." he leaned in, his lips inches from hers. "You could take a chance on me. I promise you'll like what you find."

Heat permeated her skin at his cocky demeanor. In a world where no one challenged her, here he was calling her bluff. She wanted to pull away; to tell him off, yet something about the look in his eyes made her pause. Despite the over-confidence she saw there, there was an emotion behind them she couldn't name. The longer she stared into his eyes, the more her anger shifted into something else.

Devyn's breaths quickened and she softly pressed her lips against his. Their lips moved slowly in perfect synchronicity. Devyn reached up and instinctively wrapped her arms around Coop's neck. He smiled against her, and placing his hands on her waist, pulled her closer, deepening their kiss. The heat of their actions ignited a fervent desire within them both.

Releasing her, Coop kissed the bridge of her nose. "I already know you want to take your car. So grab it, and follow me," he said.

Chapter 4

"Really nice place ya got here, Coop." Devyn breathed as they stepped into his home. It was an elegant single-detached house, surrounded by beautiful trees and a stunning garden.

"Thanks," said Coop, reaching out to take her coat from her shoulders, before tossing both their coats carelessly on the plush, upholstered entryway way bench.

Devyn reached up to carefully remove his glasses, placing them in his breast pocket. "Show me the bedroom?" she purred, eyes aflame with desire for him.

Without uttering a single word, Coop swept up her delicate frame in his strong arms and planted a fervent kiss on her lips. She wrapped her legs around him, and the warmth of his body against her sent Devyn's heart racing in her chest. The world seemed to melt around them. They paid no mind to the tables they hit nor the trinkets that clattered to the floor at the force of their passion, as they made their way through the house. With his unwavering embrace, Coop took her up the stairs. He opened the bedroom door and set her down.

Pausing to look around the room, Devyn couldn't help but feel a sense of awe at the place. The bedroom was spacious and beautifully decorated with high ceilings and large windows that allowed for sunlight, and in this case moonlight, to stream in. The walls were adorned with tasteful art and the furniture was elegant and opulent, reflecting Coop's wealth and refined taste.

Her eyes were drawn to the emperor bed, draped in luxurious silks and soft linens, situated against the wall. As she took in the room, Devyn's gaze eventually fell upon the man who had brought her there.

"That's a huge bed," she said, gesturing at the massive emperor bed situated against the wall. "Why is it double-bolted?"

"I toss and turn in my sleep," Coop replied simply. Devyn looked like she wanted to pry further so Coop reached out, cradling her delicate face in his hands, and pressed his lips against hers in a passionate kiss. Successfully distracted, she kissed back with an enthusiasm that matched his own. Coop kept their lips locked as he reached down and unbuttoned his jeans.

Impatient, Devyn moved his hands and helped him out of his boxer briefs herself. Her fingers closed around his hardening manhood, eliciting a deep moan of pleasure from him that made her smile inside. She tugged him towards her, wrapping her lips around his length and taking him into her mouth.

"Shit ..." Coop gasped, breaths quickening as he felt her tongue swirl around the length of him and she pulled him in deeper. He moaned with pleasure as Devyn ran her tongue around the sensitive tip of his shaft, saliva trickling down her chin. Coop tilted his head back, relishing the sensation, breaths deepening. Not wanting to finish too soon, he pulled her up.

Devyn grabbed his hand and escorted him to the bed. Helping him out of the rest of his clothes, she pushed him onto the large bed.

"Your enthusiasm's appreciated," Coop breathed, his eyes flitting over Devyn's body, as he leaned back to rest on his forearms. "But do you always need to be the one in control?" he asked, his voice dripping with amusement.

Devyn flashed him an attractive smile, full of a wild kind of promise. "Mhm." She parted her lips and stepped out of her red dress, swaying towards him. He hungrily devoured her dark complexion with his eyes, an alluring contrast against her white lace lingerie. Devyn threw herself atop of Coop, exploring his powerful shoulders with her fingertips as her lips feverishly tasted his. A familiar heat began to pool in her stomach as Coop's hot lips tantalized her, begging for her surrender. Suddenly, a low growl escaped Coop's lips as he flipped her beneath him.

Devyn gasped in both surprise and delight, completely caught off guard. "Wha —"

Coop trapped her in his strong grip, pinning her wrists against the soft sheets. His intense gaze sent a shiver of passion down her spine. The handsome man leaned over and whispered into her ear in a voice as thick and velvety as honey, "Well, not tonight."

He released her hands and trailed gentle kisses from her mouth to her neck, while he slipped a hand beneath her and deftly unhooked her bra with one hand; tossing it to the hardwood floor.

The feel of his lips sent shivers of delight through Devyn's body, as they scorched a path across her neck and behind her ears. Coop made quick work of her lace panties, before his strong hands cupped and fondled her perky, full breasts, sending cascades of pleasure down Devyn's spine with each gentle squeeze. Coop soon replaced his hands with his mouth, tongue swirling around her nipples. Helplessly, she felt her body uncontrollably responding to his every caress. Devyn writhed beneath him, and Coop reveled in the way she panted each time he touched her. Coop kissed down her stomach and dipped his tongue into her navel. No longer able to keep it in, Devyn finally allowed a moan to escape her throat.

With the ghost of a smile on his lips, Coop opened her thighs and slowly kissed the inside of each one. "Devyn," he said as he positioned his face between her legs. "There are certain things that even *you* can't control."

"I can —" A shock of pleasure raced through Devyn as Coop's hot tongue ran over her slick folds. She jerked at the feel of his firm tongue circling her clit with expertise. She tensed as he drew it into his mouth, sucking on it lightly until her moans filled the room.

When she began to tremble, Coop knew she was close, and ceased his actions. He ran a hand through his hair, pushing strands out of his face in a seductive manner, lips wet with her juices. "You can't, but I can," he whispered.

Before she could argue, he placed his tongue between her thighs again. This time Coop dipped his tongue into her depths, before dragging it up to her clit in a single motion. Devyn felt her legs trembling as the tension inside her rose once more. Coop teased her with varying intensities, coaxing pleasure out of her until she couldn't form a sentence. Her head fell back against the pillow, and she gripped the sheets as the pressure built up inside her. Suddenly, her legs convulsed, and her eyes rolled back in sweet ecstasy.

"Fu —" she cried out in blissful release, her whole body quivering.

Coop licked his lips and smirked. Gently biting her clit, he grabbed her hands when she tried to stop him. He pinned them at her sides and ran his tongue against her once more. His movements were precise as he continued his sweet torture of her. Devyn shut her eyes, whimpering despite herself, still sensitive from her first climax. Addicted to the way she tasted; Coop's hunger was not satisfied until she had orgasmed thrice more for him.

Letting go of her hands, Coop positioned himself between her legs and his lips enveloped hers in a passionate kiss. His hands roamed her body, leaving a trail of fire everywhere they touched. "Spread your legs wider," he spoke against her mouth, and she obeyed instantly.

Devyn felt his manhood press against her heat and she moaned, anticipating what would come. Coop planted gentle kisses along her neck as he entered her depths in a maddeningly slow manner. Devyn's breaths quickened as she took in each inch of him, until he was fully inside her. She knew Coop was big but his length and thickness still surprised her. He continued to kiss her neck, having ceased any other movements, as if waiting for her to adjust to his size.

"Are you all right?" he spoke against her skin after a moment, when her breathing seemed to calm.

In response, Devyn bucked up against him, encouraging him to start moving. At first Coop's strokes were slow and torturous. She bit into his shoulder as the discomfort began to fade and soon gave way to sparks of pleasure. She felt him shift positions above her, angling his hips so that every stroke brushed against a bundle of nerves that drove Devyn wild. He picked up speed and all she could do was dig her nails into his back and hold on.

At the moment when her eyelids fluttered closed, she heard him softly say, "No, stay with me, Devyn. I want to see you." He gently intertwined their fingers and watched her expressions as she experienced bliss.

Coop caressed the side of her face and deepened his stroke. "Does that feel good?" he asked, and she nodded. "Then tell me it does. I need to hear you say it."

His thrusts became deeper, and he angled himself so that he was directly hitting that sensitive bundle of nerves inside with every thrust of his thick, long member. "Yes, Coop!" she said through a trembling breath. "It feels good. D-don't stop."

The hazel of his eyes seemed to change right in front of her to a piercing silver. An unmistakable, low growl escaped his throat and he flipped her on her side, entering her again. Her back against his chest, Coop craned her neck and made her look at him. Not only were his actions possessive, but he looked almost feral. "God, you're so beautiful. Just perfect," he said, and kissed her with an urgency that sent heat through her entire body. Lifting her leg and placing it on his forearm, Coop increased the pace and vigor of his thrust. Feeling his fingers dig into the flesh of her thigh, a little pain mixed with all the pleasure, made Devyn moan aloud once more.

"Enjoy it," he coaxed, knowing she was close again. Her body shook, and he kissed her neck. "You got this," he whispered and stroked deeper inside her. "I know you got this because I got you. I got you until you stop wanting me, though I hope that's never the case." Mascara tears stained her face as she felt herself lose control. Craning her neck again, Coop kissed her passionately as her explosive climax caused him to release. Repositioning her to face him, Coop held her close and rubbed her back. "Are you alright?"

Flustered, but deeply satisfied, she tried to collect herself. "Yes," she answered, struggling to look into his eyes now for some reason. "I'm alright. ... This is just new for me."

"Me too," he admitted, before lifting her chin with a finger, forcing her to meet his gaze. "But I'm happy about it." He kissed the top of her head. "I'm happy about you, and where this could go."

Devyn's mind reeled as she thought about the entire night. Coop was unlike anyone she'd ever met. He was captivating, endearing, witty, and made her feel excitement towards a relationship once more - something she hadn't realized was absent from her life the past few years. She rotated her body so that they were spooning properly, her back against his solid frame. Sleepily, Coop pulled the plush, laundry-fresh covers of his bed over them, and stroked her hair. Devyn's gaze drifted to the cold, foggy glass of the large, bedroom window. For a moment, she allowed herself to imagine what could potentially be between them.

Things like this don't happen to people like me. She reminded herself as she closed her eyes, relaxing under his calming touches. Holding back her tears, she forced herself to push thoughts of what could be from her mind.

3:00 AM

Devyn blinked, scanning the unfamiliar room. Feeling a muscular arm draped around her body, she went frigid.

Fuck! When did I fall asleep?!

It was her number one rule: never drop her guard in unknown places. She cursed under her breath at the fact she'd opted to leave any source of protection she had in the car. It was a costly mistake, and she didn't make mistakes. Cautiously, she turned over and looked at Coop. He snored lightly in his sleep.

Moments of their night flashed in her mind, and she felt a blush heat her cheeks. He'd devoured every inch of her, leaving her body still in slight orgasmic shock even hours later. She reached out and her hand mere inches from his handsome face as if to touch his smooth cheek. Just as quickly, she recoiled.

What is the matter with you?! she chastised herself.

He smiled in his sleep and pulled her closer, and she closed her eyes. Waiting for his grasp to loosen, she slipped out of his arms. Quietly, she gathered her clothes and tiptoed from the bed. Exhaling sharply, she turned to sneak one more look at him.

"Shit!" she swore, seeing Coop sitting up, wide awake in the bed, watching her intently.

He stood, still gloriously naked from last night, and Devyn's clothes fell from her hands to her dismay. He strode toward her, closing the distance between them in a few strides. Now, standing in front of her, he cocked his head, brows furrowed and mouth downturned in what could easily be described as a scowl.

"Dev?" he spoke low-voiced. "Where do you think you're going?"

Chapter 5

This was the first time she had ever seen him truly angry. It was both intimidating and arousing.

"I'm not an expert on this type of thing," he started with a seething tone. "But isn't it proper to leave cash on the nightstand before leaving?"

Devyn felt a pang of guilt at the thought of hurting Coop. She spoke up, her voice tinged with remorse, "It's not like that. I just don't spend the night."

He chuckled mirthlessly. "Right, that's so much better."

"Oh please," she retorted, unable to hold back her own anger. "If we were at my house you would have long disappeared by now."

Her words seemed to strike something in him. His posture sagged and he spoke softer now.

"Devyn, if we were at your place, I'd be thinking the same thing I'm thinking now; what to make you for breakfast."

She huffed not wanting to believe it, and he sighed heavily, running a hand through his now disheveled hair. "What the hell happened to you? I understand that this is moving fast, but why can't you just trust that whatever I said last night, I still mean this morning?" His tone became gentle, grew quieter. "As infuriating as you can be, I like you a lot, and I *know* you feel the same."

Devyn had a particular talent for sabotaging relationships before they ever had a chance to blossom into something more, to spare herself from inevitable disappointment. It was something she'd had lots of experience with, and was beginning to deploy some of her top methods now. "Coop, I'm not the kind of person you want to get involved with."

He walked towards her, lifting his hand to touch her cheek softly. "How about letting me decide that." He paused, then said, "It's alright to breathe around me. I know the world demands you be strong all the time, but ... I don't." Her bottom lip quivered slightly. She tried to turn her face, but he wouldn't let her. "Please stay. If later you want to run for the hills, I won't bother you again."

The sincerity in his eyes made her heart quicken.

"Okay," she relented. "I'll try."

"That's all I ask." Escorting her back to the bed, he climbed inside and patted the pillow beside him. "Back to your side. This pillow is yours. I can see the drool on it."

"I do *not* drool," Devyn protested, climbing into the bed next to him.

He kissed her cheek. "You do, and since I have to sleep in the wet spot, I call this a fair trade." Her face flushed, and he laughed. "I'm only teasing. I consider it a great start."

"Start of what?"

"Something really special."

The moonlight from the window illuminated his eyes like two beacons of silver light. Devyn's breath caught in her throat at their beauty. "Your eyes look almost silver," she whispered in awe. His irises seemed to glow brighter at her words.

Climbing on top of her, Coop positioned himself between her thighs. Strands of his hair cascaded over his face, and his feral look returned. She reached up, arms roaming over his cheeks and down his neck to the solid wall of muscle on his chest and abs. Her hands continued to roam down his sides to his firm, round ass.

Has he always been so buff? She wondered. Devyn noted that he felt warmer than usual as well.

"There's something about you that makes me lose control," he said in a rough, low morning voice that ignited a heat within her lower stomach. She could feel his thick manhood hardening against her thigh and she thrust her hips gently against him. Her own primal instincts ignited.

She widened her legs, and he groaned. "Then don't hold back," she told him with a lust-filled stare.

He didn't need to be asked twice.

Devyn barely had time to brace herself before he plunged himself into her depths with an intensity that made her gasp. In his minotaur form, Coop's masculinity overflowed, creating a more intense longing for him in Devyn. His fur was soft against her skin, his arm and leg muscles bulging and his abs even firmer. His member was no exception to his transformation - the head had grown longer and the shaft thicker, much like a bull's.

Yet, even with these physical changes, Coop moved with such precision and control, expertly guiding his hips in a way that stroked her deepest places, and made her juices flow. She could only toss her head back, moaning, as his pace quickened and he ravished her completely. The intensity mounted with each passing second.

Her inner muscles ached delicately from being stretched and used so intensely, and she clawed at his shoulders without thought. The orgasmic tension grew until it crashed over her like a tsunami, leaving her breathless and shaking. She felt him release deep inside her, pumping until he was spent and satisfied.

They collapsed onto each other in a tangled heap, panting from the effort of their lovemaking session. Coop carefully withdrew himself from her and rolled her atop himself. Absentmindedly, he stroked his claw-like nails gently over her back, drawng calming circles against her sweat-soaked brown skin, as her head lay against his broad chest.

"What we share, I don't want to have with anyone else," he told her.

Devyn could feel his heart beating in time with her own.

"Me too," she spoke softly.

She closed her eyes, feeling sleepy and, for once in a long time, at peace. She wrapped her arm tightly around Coop's waist, and held him close to her, not wanting to let go yet.

Two Weeks Later - Night

Devyn stood twirling a switchblade between her hands with expertise.

"Well, gentlemen," she said in a pleasant tone as she surveyed the two human traffickers kneeling with their arms and legs bound by tightly knotted ropes in the small, dank room. "Since you refuse to tell us anything else about your crime ring, I guess we're done here. Wouldn't you say?"

Bound by perfectly tied ropes, and mouths gagged, the two gruff-looking men avoided her gaze. The bald one at least looked remorseful, but the middle-aged, bearded man's head shot up suddenly and he glared defiantly back at her.

He mumbled something that was obstructed by his gag. Devyn stepped closer and loosened the cloth so he could speak.

"Do you have anything else to say?" she asked.

"We've already told you everything we know," he spat.

"Which is?"

"We've only been in the business a few months now. Sold only three women so far; the dead one we mentioned earlier and two others."

"Where are they? Who did you sell them to?"

"They were bought and transported out of state weeks ago. And we never got the names of the guys we sold them to. We communicated over Whosapp, with usernames and disposable phone numbers. How many times we gotta tell you this? Dumb bitch," he whispered the last bit under his breath.

His bald partner lowered his head, but his shoulders rose and fell in a silent laugh.

Devyn rolled her eyes. "Okay, yeah, fuck this. I have plans and this is taking too long. Trixie, if you please."

Trixie stepped up and brandished a knife of her own. Reaching up, she roughly grabbed the man's hair and yanked his head back.

"There's a special place in hell for people like you," said Devyn, walking into his line of sight. His eyes trailed her as hatred radiated off of him. Trixie watched Devyn for a different reason; she was waiting for her sign. Devyn gave it to her with a simple nod.

With an expert flick of her wrist, Trixie sliced a clean line across the man's neck. Devyn walked behind his bald companion, who was now thrashing around as much as the ropes would allow, yelling and screaming.

Devyn ignored him, she was very good at ignoring the pleas of murderers, she'd had lots of practice. The bald man met a similar fate to his partner when Devyn gripped his jaw, roughly tilted back his head and swiftly cut into his throat. Both men lay motionless in seconds, their lifeblood slowly pooling into the drains below them.

"May you think of me often as you all rot together," said Devyn to their lifeless bodies, before turning away to look at Trixie who was smirking at her.

"We love a good send-off," Trixie said, cleaning the blade with a cloth she kept in the back pocket of her cutting trousers. "Of all the things you've ever taught me, this lesson was my favorite one."

"Which lesson?" Devyn asked her. She gave Trixie so many "lessons," she occasionally forget them herself.

"'Only do enough to ensure they're dead. Any more suggests rage and passion, which gets most people caught.' It's hard sometimes to stick to the rule, though. Those two sicken me."

"Tell me about it, but it's important that we do follow that rule. I've had my share of close calls when I've gone too far." Devyn collected her things. "You gonna be alright?"

"Girl, you know clean-up is my specialty. This place will be spotless by the time you see it next, and Felix will be here soon to gather the bodies."

Devyn smiled. "Well, it's clear you don't need me anymore. Seriously though, you're better than anyone I've ever met, Trixie. Thank you for always having my back."

Trixie basked in the praise. "I learned from the best," she said simply, never one to gloat. "Plus, I wouldn't want you to miss spending time with your man," she added with a cheeky smile.

"How many times do I have to tell you we are *not* together?"

"If he spoils you, and sends you home walking funny, honey, *that's* your man. Not to mention every time I've seen him, he's completely starry-eyed over you."

Devyn couldn't hide her smile at the thought of Coop. It had only been two weeks, but he had kept his word in every way possible. Whether it was extravagant dinners, or movie nights in, there wasn't one moment that she'd felt like she wasn't his primary focus. There was one thing that was still bothering her, though.

"I still can't find anything detailed about him," Devyn mused aloud. "All anyone seems to know is that he's rich, and nice. ...I don't like it. Anyone who doesn't have a footprint, doesn't have one for a *reason*."

"You mean like *you*?" Trixie asked. Devyn rolled her eyes. "I'm just saying, your actual record stops after you moved away from your foster parents. I only know about your past because you told me."

"I *had* to conceal my past to protect them. *You* know that," Devyn retorted.

"So there you have it - you're as mysterious as he is," Trixie said, turning on the hose mounted on the wall.

"You got me there," Devyn said, "but that's not going to stop me from finding out more."

"Nothing wrong with getting your hands wet - figuratively and literally," she added suggestively.

They shared a laugh. Devyn heard the chime of a phone notification. "Shit. That's probably him now. I'm going to be late."

"Get going," Trixie said, and Devyn bustled through the door. When she entered the hallway, she found the trafficking victim's grieving husband waiting there. He looked up when she approached him, eyes bleak with despair.

"It's done," she told him softly.

He exhaled deeply, a sense of relief filling him. "You guys were my last resort to get the people responsible. The police kept dragging their feet and making excuses. I-I don't know how to thank you. My wife can finally rest in peace." Tears filled his eyes. "I lost my love over the greed and lack of human compassion those people have. It's disgusting how some people are in this world."

Devyn felt his loss, but forced a reassuringly smile and placed a hand upon his trembling shoulder. "That's why we're here, Alfred."

He gave her a look of gratitude, although his expression soon shifted back to one of anxiety.

"What's wrong?" Devyn asked, concerned.

"That detective has been going around town asking questions about missing criminals again."

"He's *always* asking questions."

"Not like these," said Alfred. "The questions are no longer as harmless as they used to be. He may not overtly make threats, but we can tell they're there. Even if it's just implied."

Her eyes darkened. "I'll take care of it. Don't worry. None of this will trace back to you ... or me," she added.

"Thank you, but please be careful. This community cares about you and what you stand for so much. If there ever came a reason, we would lie down our lives to save yours."

"If there ever came a reason, I would die before I ever asked you to."

Alfred fixed Devyn with a serious look. "We would die before you ever could."

Chapter 6

Coop's face shone with a luminous joy as Devyn stepped through the door.

"Sorry I'm late," she said, pressing her lips to his. "It took longer than I thought."

"It's all right. I'm just glad you made it. I've missed you."

"Is that so?" she quipped, her lips forming a sly grin. "Prove it."

He answered her challenge with a ravishing kiss, as he held her in an embrace that was both tender and strong. She melted against him, sighing in contentment. Smoothly, his hands slid down her body, appreciating her curves and eliciting muffled sighs of pleasure from her. His touch finally settled upon her behind, and he squeezed gently before pulling away to look at her, eyes smoldering as he drank in the sight of her.

"I did miss you," Coop repeated, voice husky.

"I missed you too," she whispered earnestly, face burning as her hands roamed over his chest.

With a gentle smile, Coop took her hand and guided her to the living room. There on the table was a beautiful spread of gourmet hors d'oeuvres that were sure to make any foodie jealous. Devyn gasped audibly at the sight of it all.

"Everything looks so good."

"I wish I could say this was my own work, but I'm no master chef."

"Asterions?" She guessed with amusement in her tone.

"The perks of being a restaurant owner," he grinned, delighted to hear Devyn laugh. "Let's eat to our heart's content and then move on to even better things."

She quirked an eyebrow. "You mean there's more than just an amazing meal?"

He laughed good-naturedly. "Of course! What kind of boyfriend do you take me for?"

She raised a brow. "*Boyfriend*, huh?"

Coop scratched his head. "Hmm. It does sound a little immature. *Manfriend*? No, that somehow sounds worse."

Devyn laughed at his flustered state. "Boyfriend is fine. Real smooth title grab, by the way."

"I am a man who knows what he wants," he said proudly. "And I've decided that I'm going to let you, let me ask, to be your boyfriend."

Pulling him to her, she gave him a gentle kiss. "I accept, arrogance and all."

After savoring their meal, Coop guided Devyn to the bathroom and instructed her to shower before meeting him in the bedroom. Coop's smoldering gaze welcomed hers when she arrived at the threshold of his room wrapped in a large, fluffy towel. He was scantily clad only in white silk boxers - that left little to the imagination - his tanned, tone frame illuminated by the glow of the scented candles.

"I like where this is going," she flirted, admiring him, as she sucked in a tantalizing breath.

"Get your mind out of the gutter," Coop retorted playfully, motioning her closer but his eyes roamed over her glistening, brown skin just the same. "Take off the towel and lay on the bed on your stomach." She obeyed without question.

Reaching for a bottle of warmed body oil, he began to massage her back in gentle strokes. "I know you've been so tense lately. I wanted to help."

Devyn moaned at the exquisite sensation of his touch as the pressure of his fingers increased and the tension melted away from her body. "That feels good," she murmured with pleasure, biting the side of her lip as he continued to knead her waist, buttocks, and legs. Her boyfriend left nothing untouched.

"Turn over," he demanded, voice low and deep, and gave her butt a playful slap that made her jump a little. She complied and they locked eyes. Coop was barely able to conceal his desire as he admired her beauty. Once again, for a split second, his eyes seemed to flash silver.

I didn't imagine it, his eye color does change! She thought.

Coop massaged from her neck to her breasts. Her nipples hardened, and he leaned down and caught each between his teeth.

"Oh..."

He continued his massage down her stomach, moving lower until he landed between her thighs. Carefully, he massaged the folds of her femininity. Hearing her moan, he slipped two fingers inside of her. She arched her back and rolled against his fingers as he stroked her sweet spot. Removing his fingers, and feeling bolder now, he dove his tongue into her wetness, drawing moans from deep within her chest as her hands found purchase in his hair.

Coop circled her clit with his tongue, before taking it in his warm mouth and humming. The vibrations tore through Devyn, and she rolled her hips upward, greedy for more of the delicious sensation.

"You're going to make me cum..." she gasped a few moments later, feeling her climax approaching.

He jerked her closer to him and continued to stimulate her clit, alternating between driving his tongue deep inside her. Her legs shook as she cried out his name and came undone all around him - her juices soaking the towels beneath her.

Coop joined her on his bed, pulled her close, and let her catch her breath. Eventually, when her breathing had calmed somewhat, he whispered, "Feeling better?"

She looked up at him in the warm afterglow. "That was amazing...this entire afternoon has been thoughtful and amazing." She reached up to touch his neck, hand moving over his sharp jawline before gently cupping his cheek. "Thank you."

He held the hand against his cheek, adjusting it slightly to kiss her wrist. "You deserve it and more."

"Tell me a secret," Devyn said suddenly.

He quirked a brow. "A secret?"

"Yes. Something that no one knows about you."

Coop paused for a moment in thought. "I wish I was closer with my family," he said. "I wish I could live up to the expectations that they have for me."

"Why can't you?"

"Because I'm not brave enough. The things they want me to do... are meant for someone else."

Devyn rubbed his arm, and he relaxed under her touch. "Do you think you could ever be brave enough?"

"I don't know. I'd love to be, though. I can conquer everything in my life. Everything except what matters most; the expectations of those who mean the most to me. A lot of people think I turned my back on them, when in reality, I just don't think I'm good enough to be the person they want me to be." He kissed her cheek. "I've never told anyone that."

"Thank you for telling me." She fiddled with a loose thread on the bedsheet. "I know what you mean, by the way."

He looked at her curiously. "Do you now?"

"Yeah. For me, it was my sister, Bria. She died two years ago, and there isn't a day that I don't feel like I failed her."

"Why?"

"Because I was so stuck on myself, I didn't see that she needed me until it was too late. We both were products of the foster care system, but she came out with more scars than I realized. I wish I had heard her cries for help sooner, but I put my career and everything above her. So, she sought solace in someone else who harmed her. A cop's brother, Rayes, who used her pain against her. He became obsessed with her, and when she tried to break free, he kidnapped her."

Devyn wiped her eyes. "I searched everywhere for her, but it was like they were ghosts ... and by the time I found her, it was too late. My little sister, dead and tossed in the dumpster like she was garbage by a man who had the law on his side." Coop could feel her anger, and he held her tighter. "I've done some digging and learned my sister wasn't the only girlfriend of his who mysteriously died during his brother's time on the police force."

"Sounds like he was confident he'd never go down for any of the deaths with a cop in the family," Coop pitched in.

"Yeah," she agreed. "Not long after that, he went missing without a trace. His family eventually concluded that he had perished and the police force his brother worked for, organized a memorial service in his honor since they were all very close. Of course, the tragedy of losing him overshadowed my sister's case, and she was quickly forgotten. His brother left the force shortly afterward, to protect himself from being implicated in the future."

"I'm so sorry, Devyn."

She nodded. "I get what it's like to feel the pain of letting your family down, but as much as you believe you aren't brave Coop, I believe in you." She looked up at him. "I don't trust many people, but I trust *you*, and you opened up to me, which makes you brave in my eyes. Few people can share their pain with others. So I truly appreciate you trusting me enough to share." His intense gaze made her hide her face. "Ah, did I make it weird?"

"No...you're just...I..." he kissed her, and she melted in his arms. "I've never met anyone like you."

"Likewise."

They snuggled close, their minds on the others' admission. Feeling at peace, they soon fell asleep.

What the hell is that?

Devyn shifted in her sleep at the feel of something damp on her shoulder. Reaching behind her, her eyes shot open as she made out the shape of a cold snout. She kicked her legs, and fur hit her skin. Hardened hooves rubbed against her feet, locking her in place. Trembling, she moved her hand upward and grabbed a sharp horn.

"Baby, can you stop messing with my horns? It's turning me on. You keep doing that, and we'll be at it all morning."

Devyn belted a scream, "Ahhhh!"

Coop jolted awake. It only took him a few seconds to register what was happening. His own voice tore through the room, "Ahhhh!" he roared as his now huge, animal-like frame tumbled from the bed.

Chapter 7

Coop hit the floor hard. Springing to his feet, he searched for Devyn. "Wait! I can explain!" he shouted as she bolted for the door.

"Stay away from me!" She reached into her purse, and his eyes widened when she pointed a large knife at him.

"Where the hell did you get a machete?! And why is it in your purse?!"

"What the hell are you?!" she demanded, ignoring his question.

"Answer me first! Where the hell did you get a machete?!"

"It was a gift! You never know what creeps are out here! I'm always prepared!"

He cocked his head to the side. "Who gets someone a machete as a gift?"

"Don't you *dare* judge my friend. I'll have you know it's one of the best gifts I've ever received. Trixie can be very thoughtful ... wait, what am I saying? What the hell are you?!"

Coop, flustered by the situation, attempted to reason with her. "Look, I know this is a lot to process, but please, just let me explain." He warily stepped toward her, but in his panic, his head collided with a hanging lamp, and he fell sideways into the bedroom wall where his left horn became lodged.

"Ow!" he cried out miserably. He could see Devyn taking a few steps back. "H-hang on! Please, Devyn, don't go!" Freeing himself from the drywall, and leaving shattered plaster in his wake, he stumbled backward, tripping over himself and bumping his hoof against the nightstand. He grabbed his sore hoof and wailed in pain. "Fucking hell!" Struggling to stand again, only to step on his long tail, Coop emitted a sharp yelp of pain, "Ow! Ow! Dammit!"

Unable to combat any more catastrophic falls or injuries, Coop crashed onto his bed and let out an exhausted huff. "Oh forget it. At this rate, you won't have to decapitate me. Just give me another minute and I'll end up taking out myself."

Devyn took one look at the pout on his animal-like face and saw Coop right through it. Unable to hold it in, she dropped the machete and her laughter filled the air. The entire situation was utterly ridiculous. Each part of the damaged room made her laugh until she couldn't breathe. Wiping her teary eyes, she laughed harder when she realized his pout had turned into a scowl. "I have no idea what's going on, but that was pure comedy. I'm terrified, but I have to stay and hear this," she said.

"It isn't funny!" he shouted, irritated. "I could have really hurt myself." His sulkiness, despite his stature, only succeeded in tickling Devyn's funny bone further.

"Your head almost touches the ceiling," she chortled, "and yet here you are, getting your butt handed to you by your own house. I'm sorry, but it's pretty hilarious." Taking a breath, she cast him a gentle look.

Coop's eyes softened. "You don't have to be afraid of me," he said quietly. "I may look different, but I'm still me."

"Still you," Devyn repeated softly. Studying him for a moment, she took in his snout, fur-covered face, silver eyes, long fangs and ears, massive horns, his large and muscular build covered in soft-looking fur from the waist down, his tail and hooved feet. "But, just, what exactly *are* you?" she whispered.

He hung his head, unable to meet her gaze. He spoke quietly, "A minotaur."

"T-that's not possible. Minotaurs - shifters - don't exist." But she sounded unsure of herself. How could she make such a definitive claim when he was sitting right there? When she was looking right at him – a minotaur shifter? Clearly, her beliefs were untrue.

He answered her silent thought rather simply. "We do. Many supernaturals are living among humankind. You just don't realize it because you're programmed to believe the Supernatural is fictional. That and we manage to blend in - *cloaking* is what I've heard some call it. Also, the veil between our world and yours is thin, so we cross over pretty frequently. Some of us establish partial lives here, and some of us opt to stay here indefinitely."

Devyn squeezed her eyes shut in a desperate attempt to wake up from what felt like a fever dream — of course, it didn't work.

"Why?" she asked him finally, "Why stay in this world? It's terrible here." She spoke the last part quietly, thinking of all the criminals she and her crew had to take off the streets each year. She thought of all the victims these criminals left in their wake. Surely any world was better than this one, where evil acts too often went unpunished and bad people were always protected.

Coop lifted his broad shoulders in a shrug, "I've been told there are some things worth fighting for in this world. Things that hold such significance we could even begin to fathom what life would be like without them. It took me a while to understand this." He turned to look at her, "... but, I get it now." She averted her eyes, and he sighed. "I didn't mean to scare you – I shifted in my sleep."

"Were you ever gonna tell me you were a minotaur?" she whispered.

Coop shook his head, and her heart dropped. "Call me a coward, but I couldn't bear the thought of you looking at me like you are now. I can control when I change... usually. I guess I just got too comfortable around you. The things we talked about meant a lot to me. It made me feel..."

"Safe," she murmured.

"*Yes*," he confirmed and she felt deep relief at this. "I feel that between us is a safe space. But, you never have to see this side of me again. I'll make sure of it. Just ... stay."

"No!" said Devyn instantly, unable to stop herself. She couldn't stand to hear anymore. How could he even ask such a thing? "No," she said more quietly, after seeing Coop's shocked expression. "I don't want you to do that. Don't hide yourself away from me." The words left her mouth before she even realized it, but it was true. Briefly, she thought of the irony in that statement. Though Coop wasn't quite human, he wasn't the most dangerous in the room.

Filled with trepidation, she advanced towards him, and cautiously perched herself on the edge of the bed. Gently, she placed her hand upon his. Her voice was soft but resolute; "Listen to me," she started. "You'll always have a safe place with me."

Coop tenderly grasped Devyn's hand and gave it a meaningful squeeze. She noted that his skin was hotter than she remembered, yet still retained the comfort of familiarity.

Devyn thought to herself, he really was her Coop, as he had always been.

She quickly glanced around them. "I guess this explains why the bed is so huge and double-bolted." Her mouth upturned into a mischievous smile as she continued in a sly voice, "So ... does this make you a *Taurus*?" She waited for his reaction, but when he didn't smile back, she prodded him with her elbow, winking playfully. "I'm only joking."

Finally, reluctantly, Coop cracked a small smile. "I know." The air between them seemed to still, until he offered up something to help it flow once more. "I'm a Gemini by the way."

At this Devyn looked at him in amusement, "That was gonna be my second guess."

"Liar," said Coop with a laugh.

"Am not," Devyn protested banteringly. "Anyway, Geminis and Libras are supposed to be a great match."

"Ah, so you *are* a Libra. I figured as much," Coop stated with an air of confidence, causing Devyn to raise an eyebrow in surprise.

"You did? How?"

The minotaur shifter merely smiled at her enigmatically. "Call it a hunch."

A peaceful hush descended upon them and Devyn reached out, fingers gently grazing across Coop's still human torso, tracing over hard abs. His eyes closed as she continued her journey up to the soft fur on his face.

Removing the drywall remnants from it, she smiled. "Much better."

"Thank you."

"You're welcome." She ran her hands over his horns, and he instantly froze.

"Don't," he said, harshly, recoiling.

"Don't tell me what to do." She ran her hands over the deep-rooted scars on them. "Do these hurt?" Devyn whispered, "They look like they hurt."

He opened his eyes and saw her bottom lip trembling. "Not anymore," he assured her.

She looked from the thick rope of his tail and rubbed his horns again. Coop's brows furrowed, and he inhaled sharply trying to bear it but failing.

"I can't take you touching me," he said honestly.

"Why not? Are they sensitive?"

Coop shifted into his complete human form, but Devyn noticed his eye color remained silver. "Because I don't let anyone get this close. And yet, since the moment I saw you, I wanted you near me."

Devyn's expression softened at this. "Me too. I don't want you to hide from me. I want you to be *you*." Devyn smiled, feeling her cheeks grow warm. "I like looking at you either way."

Coop clashed their lips in a passionate kiss that sent electricity through them both. "God, you're perfect. You're absolutely perfect," he murmured and kissed her again. Hearing his sincere words, Devyn broke their kiss and backed away. Her face crumbled and her shoulders shook as dread filled her. "What's wrong, Dev?" Coop asked, his panic setting in again. "Talk to me."

She shook her head. "I'm not perfect," she whispered. "Not at all. I've done awful things."

Coop looked around the room, and then down at his own hands. "I don't think there is anything you could tell me that would trump what you just witnessed."

"No Coop, there is. I'm not normal. What I do for work isn't normal, and what's worse is that I don't feel bad about it, which makes me even more messed up. That's why I had to tell you. You said this was a safe place and I hope you meant it."

"I did, but Devyn, you don't have to tell me anything."

"Yes, I do. If you really want me, then you need to know the truth about what I am. I was late because I slashed a man's throat tonight." His eyes widened, and she went on. "But that's not even the worst thing I've done. You remember the cop's brother who I told you kidnapped and killed my sister? His name was Rayes. And I left out that he was my first kill. He inspired my desire to keep dangerous criminals off the streets because the criminal legal system keeps failing victims and their families. That man's cop brother and his buddies searched everywhere for his body without realizing they had it all along."

"What does that mean?" he asked, somehow already knowing the answer.

She let out a breath and stared blankly forward. "It means they couldn't find it because I had him feed to pigs that were served as dishes at his memorial."

Chapter 8

Coop moved away from her. "What did you say?"

"You heard me. I'm a vigilante that fed a man to his own corrupt brother and his friends." She could feel her fists trembling, trying to hold in the rush of overwhelming emotions growing within her. "So, tell me, still think you wanna get involved with someone like me?" His silence made her chuckle. "That's what I thought. I'll get out of your hair...fur...I'll leave." She stood up and began to head towards the bedroom door, but a gentle hand on her wrist stopped her in her tracks.

"No. Wait. I'm sorry. I just didn't know what to say. I still don't."

"I get it. All I ask is that you don't tell. Not for me, but for the community I protect."

"I won't. But Devyn, there has to be another way..."

"If there was, do you think I would do this? I look out for people who can't look out for themselves. People like my sister, who deserved justice but were forgotten instead. He took her from me, and they still let him go. I don't think so; I know it. I was given evidence of a cover-up from two rookie cops who accidentally uncovered the truth and had been threatened that their families would be killed if they told, but they did anyway. To add insult to injury, his brother convinced his entire department to frame it like my sister wasn't a victim of domestic violence. They whipped up the story that she was just an irresponsible party girl, who went out on a drug binge one night, and was attacked by a drifter. Meanwhile, they claimed Rayes died in an unrelated incident."

Coop listened intently, as she went on.

"But Rayes had an obsession with women. It was his downfall. All it took was some light flirting to get him to believe I wanted him. You should have seen his face when he came to our meetup spot and realized I wasn't alone. His fear when we surrounded him is something I'll never forget."

"What happened?" asked Coop, already dreading the answer.

"The plan was never to feed him to animals. But my rage took over me, and I stabbed him so many times that I knew I'd made myself a primary suspect in his murder. Yet, everyone there that night was so grateful he wasn't a threat to the community anymore. One man, a pig farmer, suggested we feed his body to a few of his most ravenous pigs. Then he butchered them, and cooked them in time for Rayes' memorial. There they served a pig roast, barbecue ribs, and a stew. I made sure to attend so I could watch his brother, and all the people who helped him escape a murder sentence, hide what we'd done. I killed Rayes, and the community helped me cover it up. Since then, I promised myself I'd look out for them."

Her lips lifted into a sad smile and her passion surged. "You want to know the truth about this town? There is pure evil here, and those who are supposed to protect it – cops, judges, lawyers – are at the forefront. But don't get me wrong, there are still some good ones in those roles. I defend them and I'd never hurt anyone who didn't deserve it. You can judge me all you want, but if you think I'm going to sit by and let someone who harmed an innocent person walk free, you're sadly mistaken."

Coop saw her fists clench tighter. Her body was rigid, and she looked as though she'd attack him should he take a step closer. "Come here," he said, extending his hand to her, but she didn't move.

"No," she said numbly. "I want to leave."

"Come here, Devyn," he insisted with more command in his voice this time.

She closed her eyes and shook her head, pain clear in her expression. "No," she said in a soft voice. "I can see it on your face. You know I'm the only monster here. Just let me leave."

"You're not going anywhere." He approached her and pulled her into his strong embrace. "I'm not letting you leave me," he whispered into her hair. He heard her sob, and he held her tighter. "I don't think you're a monster. You're perfect. Absolutely perfect." He picked her up and carried her to bed. Laying her down, he joined her and held her close. She snuggled into him, and the heat of her anger dissipated.

"I'm not sorry for the things I've done," she spoke after a moment, looking up at him defiantly, though tears filled her eyes.

"I would never ask you to be," Coop replied simply and stroked her back in a soothing motion.

Within minutes, Devyn was asleep again.

Coop exhaled, his mind still reeling.

Ping.

He grabbed his phone, and his jaw tightened as he read the text on the screen. *I know she's with you. Get your ass out here. NOW!*

Slipping from the bed, Coop tugged on his clothes and made his way to the alleyway behind his house.

When he spotted the one who had texted him, a wave of anger surged through him. "What the hell do you want?" he said, fuming.

Grant's anger matched his own. "Remember who's in charge here, boy! You've been dealing with her for *weeks* now. You'd better have something to report."

Chapter 9

Coop's eyes flashed with rage as he clenched his fists, restraining his inner turmoil.

Don't shift. Coop willed himself. He inhaled deeply. "How did you know she was here?"

Grant scoffed and cocked his head to the side, his expression full of disdain. "What? Did you really think I wouldn't be keeping tabs? I shouldn't have to track you down when we had a deal. But since you stopped answering my calls, here I am," he sneered, extending his arms wide to emphasize his point.

"I stopped answering because I have nothing to say. I've *already* told you I no longer want *any* part of this!" his voice boomed.

"What the *hell* is wrong with you?" the detective demanded in rushed, quiet voice, as though to remind Coop that they were in public. "All you had to do was get her to incriminate herself. It shouldn't be that hard to get Devyn to slip up and tell you *something*. Hell, use your powers if need be!"

"I'm not doing that," Coop said evenly. "I already told you that as well."

"Oh! So you're the *King of Morals* now? Wasn't it you who made this deal? You were so down to help me turn in the little bitch in order to save yourself, remember? We're this close and now you suddenly wanna clam up?!"

"Lower your voice when you speak to me," Coop hissed venomously as his eyes slowly shifted in color, his fangs visible. He aggressively took a step forward and Grant took an involuntary step back. "And never call Devyn out of her name again," he added. "I refuse to use my powers on her, but I have no problem showing you what I can do."

Grant laughed, hiding his nervousness. "Don't threaten me with a good time, Coop."

The humor was lost on the other man. "I mean it. If you insist on going after her I'll kill you."

"That's rich coming from a mama's boy who ran away from home," Grant said, attempting to humble him, to humiliate him. "If you kill me, you'll send a beacon, and they'll find you," Grant said threateningly. "That's how you get captured, idiot. You really going to risk it?"

"Absolutely," said Coop, without missing a beat. "Learn that fast because you won't get another chance to make the same mistake."

Though he tried his best to hide it, Grant was petrified. From the moment he'd met Coop, he'd never seen the man lose his temper. This mysterious man's demeanor was only ever calm and composed. This was partly why Grant had approached Coop with the proposition in the first place. Coop's demeanor was part of what made Grant believe that he would be an obedient and controllable associate, which appealed to his own craving for control. That and he understood that Coop had a secret to keep, a secret Grant could blackmail him with if need be. The shifter wanted to preserve his façade of being "normal," so as not to raise suspicion.

Grant's blue eyes widened in realization. "*Shit*, you're in love with her." Seeing Coop's eyes return to their natural, hazel hue. He shook his head. "You were supposed to get her to fall in love with *you*, not the other way around. Damn it, Coop!" He began to pace back and forth, cursing under his breath.

Coop watched him anxiously, running his fingers through his hair in frustration. "You think I planned for this to happen?"

Grant stopped pacing and threw him a disgusted look. "And what do you think will happen when she finds out what you are? You think she's going to want you then?"

In the past Grant's words would have cut him like a knife, but knowing that someone as amazing as Devyn accepted him fully, alleviated Coop's worries. "She knows that I'm a minotaur. She accepts it."

The detective's lip curled. "But she doesn't know you betrayed her trust. She won't care that you have feelings for her when she realizes you're the reason she's going to prison for the rest of her life."

"That's not happening."

"You're right. She may get the death penalty instead."

Coop managed to stifle his anger but his blood burned in his veins. "I'm not going to let you hurt her."

Grant scoffed. "You mean worse than you did? You're kidding yourself if you think things will end with you two together. I will get the evidence I need to charge her one way or another, and when I do, I'm arresting her."

"Don't come here again," Coop said, face flushing angrily. "Do what you need to do. I'm not helping you."

Grant threw his hands up in annoyance. "Fine. Have it your way," he uttered, his words cutting through the air like a blade. He reached into his jacket, and pulled out a folder. "A piece of advice? Run back home as fast as you can."

A sense of dread came over Coop as Grant reached into the folder, gripping a stack of papers - photographs. He tossed the pictures at the minotaur shifter's feet. Gruesome black-and-white images of dead bodies - the bodies of criminals - made Coop's stomach turn. "It makes no difference if you're a minotaur or not," Grant said with a disturbed smile, and then turned away. "If Devyn finds out you double-crossed her before I can arrest her, you're done for."

Chapter 10

The shrill sound of her phone jolted Devyn awake. She groggily answered the call, her voice full of sleep.

"Hello?"

"Hey Devyn, this is Vinny. Sorry, it took so long for me to get back to you. I dropped my phone off a cliff while hiking this morning, and this amazing hiker found it and returned it to me. And guess what? It has some scratches but it still works perfectly! Can you believe that?"

"It's fine, Vin," said Devyn, not quite in the mood. "I just wish you'd have called me in the morning instead."

"Yeah, sorry about that. Your voicemail about Coop had me worried."

"Why?"

He sighed audibly. "Don't take this the wrong way, but whenever you ask questions about someone, we all know nothing good ever comes of it."

"Fair enough," she replied, chuckling. "But I only asked because he showed up out of nowhere, and I heard you were the reason behind it."

"Ah, I gotcha. Yeah, he's my silent partner in the restaurant. He's a great guy; not a snob like most rich folk in this town are, but a genuinely good guy."

"I'm learning that," she said, unable to hold in her smile.

"Do I detect a little romance going on between you two?"

"Coop is ... a really amazing person. I feel closer to him than to guys I've dated for years! I've never met anyone like him."

Vinny laughed good-naturedly before saying, "So ... you know ... er ... about him?"

Devyn caught on right away. "You can relax. I know and his secret is safe with me, Vinny."

"*That's* a relief. I didn't know how to handle that. I'd never keep anything from you, but I would never put Coop in danger either. And I know you wouldn't do anything that would lead his mother to him."

"His *mother*?" Devyn sat up in bed. "What about his mother?"

"Shit. Me and my big mouth," Vinny said, sighing. "I thought you knew about that part. Look, Coop's great, but he has some skeletons in his closet, one being his mother. She can't seem to grasp that he doesn't want to be a political leader or go through with his arranged marriage."

Devyn's eyes widened. "Political leader ... arranged marriage? What are you talking about?"

"Dev, your boy's the son of a political hero. His father was a leader who successfully changed the future of his entire nation. Thanks to him, the whole family was given something akin to royal status. His older brother has been following in his father's footsteps, and it was expected that Coop would do the same - even though he has little interest in it. His father accepted Coop's stance before he passed away. But after his father's death, Coop's mother laid the pressure on him heavy. Forcing him into a political career. Even went behind his back to plan a strategic marriage to a *Centaur* politician's daughter, she thought would help Coop gain the favor of the public. When Coop found out, that was the final straw. He ran away. The real reason he's in this town is because his mother set a two-million-dollar reward for his capture and return. Apparently, our little community isn't just a refuge for us, but for displaced supernaturals as well. His friends won't turn him in, but that doesn't mean he's not in danger if the wrong person found out."

"Thanks, Vinny," Devyn said. They spoke a bit longer but Devyn was mostly absentminded. When they finally said their goodbyes, she crashed back onto the pillow, staring blankly at the ceiling. *A political hero's son?*

Wrapped in her thoughts, Devyn didn't hear Coop enter the bedroom. "Sorry, I thought you heard me come in," he said, seeing her jump.

"Don't worry about it," she said sitting up. "Where did you go, anyway?"

"I had to take a call and I didn't want to wake you," he answered tersely. Devyn noted the lines of his face were etched deep with worry as he looked out the window.

"Is everything okay?" she asked tentatively. Silently walking over to her, he pulled her into a tight hug. Devyn wrapped her arms around his waist and held him just as tightly, resting her head on Coop's chest, she listened to his rapidly beating heart. "Hey, everything's going to be all right," she told him. She didn't know what compelled her to say that, but it just felt like what he needed to hear at the moment.

After a time Coop's voice broke the silence. "Could you ever forgive someone who betrayed your trust?" he spoke in a voice just above a whisper.

She shrugged against him, still holding him close. "I guess it depends on the infraction. I believe people can make mistakes. And, some mistakes are redeemable if the other person is actually sorry, but ... I couldn't forgive someone who would knowingly betray me for selfish reasons, especially if I've done nothing to harm them."

Coop released her. "I wouldn't forgive someone like that either."

"Yeah," she stared up at him. "I want you to know you don't have to worry about that. If anything, tonight has taught me that we are two very accepting, secret-keeping people. We may also be a little crazy," she laughed.

Coop forced himself to smile as his heart sank at Devyn's words, "Maybe more than a little." Coop couldn't help falling even deeper for Devyn. She was open with him about who she was, and she accepted the parts of Coop that he preferred to hide. It was so easy back when he knew her only through Grant's description of her - a psychopathic killer whom he could incriminate to protect himself. But now that they had connected, bonded, he realized that Devyn was the best thing to ever happen to him.

A sudden possessiveness surged through Coop and he grabbed Devyn by the waist and kissed her as if their very lives depended on it. She instantly melted into his arms, responding with equal ardor. Unsure of what the future held, Coop knew one thing for certain: he would rather die by her hands than ever leave her side.

***

A Few Days Later

"Grant," Devyn said as she once again found herself in the detective's office doorway. He looked up with an unreadable expression, and she glared. "We need to talk."

"Agreed. Close the door." She did, and he motioned for her to sit in the chair across from his desk. "I haven't had to process any bodies lately," he said as casually as one would talk about the weather. "Does that mean you're finished with your spree, my little serial killer? Finally got murdering out of your system?"

Devyn's face shifted to a leer that Grant returned with a smug look.

"I'm not here for our usual banter. I'm here because people are talking."

"What about?"

"They're saying you're harassing them, asking them inappropriate questions and not following proper procedures. In others words, you're scaring people. But they must be mistaken, right?" she tapped her nails against his desk. And her expression went grim. "Look, there's a killer out there who seems to target those who hurt others, who terrorize others. Don't you think you should be careful?"

Grant stiffened. "Wait," he said, lowering his reading glasses, his voice tight. "Are you threatening me?"

She laughed, though it didn't reach her eyes. "Of course not. Just lending you some friendly advice. Whoever this serial killer is, they clearly have a type. I wouldn't want to see you end up on their list of viable candidates." She rose to her feet. "There are a lot of good people in this community, people who just want to live in peace. It would benefit you greatly to respect that. Life would be far less comfortable for you if you don't."

"Devyn, if anyone will be uncomfortable, it's Cooper Valentin."

She froze. "What the hell do you know about him?"

"Coop? That's my guy right there," he said grinning wickedly. "We're basically buddies. And guess what? He isn't who he says he is, and that's outside of his *natural* disposition. At least when you and I spar, you know what you're up against. We don't play at being friends. With Coop, I promise you that's not the case. I suggest you direct your anger elsewhere because, believe me, I'm not the one betraying you here." He relished in Devyn's speechlessness, her pained expression.

She rose silently from the chair and walked towards the door.

Grant could almost taste his upcoming victory on his tongue. He couldn't help but rub it in, and so he called out to Devyn's retreating form. "I want you to know I'm close to bringing you down, Devyn. And I couldn't have done it without your lovable bull boy."

She clenched her teeth and slammed the door behind her.

Should have kept your end of the bargain, Coop. Screw the millions. I'll enjoy arresting her for your murder more. Grant thought as he leaned back in the chair. Grabbing his phone, he texted Coop and smiled.

Grenade headed your way, kid. Good luck with the boom - Grant.

"Wow ... yeah, you screwed yourself big time, Coop," Vinny told him over the phone. "Why didn't you tell me that obsessed detective was threatening to turn you in for the reward? I could have helped you – ."

" – I thought I could handle it, Vin, okay? If I'd known she was — "

His words died in his throat at the sound of a rattle in his living room. Coop peered out into the darkness of his hallway. "Who's out there?"

"Coop, are you okay? What's happening?" Vinny asked over the receiver.

"Someone's here," Coop whispered and quietly hung up the phone, ignoring Vinny's pleas. Rising slowly from his bed, Coop trudged down the shadowy hall, careful not to make much noise as he headed toward the source of the sound.

Standing in the entryway of the living room, Coop flipped on the light switch, and in that instant he was met with a shocking sight. Sitting on the couch, with two guns resting menacingly on the table in front of her — was Devyn.

Chapter 11

"I thought Grant would've warned you I was coming. I guess you missed it since you were talking to Vinny. Or, maybe he isn't the *buddy* you think he is."

"Buddy – ?" he mouthed, woodenly, brows furrowed in confusion.

Devyn didn't bother to explain, not in the mood to entertain his attempt at playing dumb. She ran her fingers over the guns. "Are you going to shift?" she asked.

The look on her face was so cold Coop hardly recognized her.

His voice was quiet. "No."

She peered up at him. "Good. Even if you did, there would be three bullets in you before you could make it over here. Two from me." She shaped her hand into a gun and pointed at his head. A steady red beam appeared in the middle of his forehead. "And one more. Trixie has perfect aim."

Coop raised his hands, but maintained eye contact with her. "Devyn…"

She flinched and shook her head. "You betrayed me, Cooper. Working with Detective Grant to incriminate me? *Seriously*? After everything? Was everything just apart of your ploy? Did I matter to you at all?"

Her words struck him harder than any bullet ever could. "Dev, I'm so sorry. It wasn't supposed to be this way. Of *course* you matter to me. You mean everything to me. None of what we have is part of a ploy. I called off the deal with Grant the moment I met you."

Closing her eyes, she dropped her hand. "Trix, leave. I've got this."

"I'm not leaving you here with him," Trixie said from a darkened corner.

"I'm fine," Devyn replied over her shoulder. "Get out of here. I'll call you when I'm done."

"You better," Trixie said as she slipped through the open window she had come from. Watching her leave, Devyn turned her attention back to Coop. "Did you tell him I killed Rayes?"

"No. Of course not," said Coop in a voice that held no desperation, only exhaustion. "I know you probably don't believe that, but it's true. I didn't tell him about anything you told me."

She picked up the guns. "I believe you ... which makes this worse. You're going to die for nothing." She pointed the guns at him. "Grant's cruel. He really should have told you what kind of monster you were hunting."

"You're not a monster, Devyn," Coop could not help but correct her. "You're someone who cares and protects others. You're perfect. Absolutely perfe —"

"Shut up!" Devyn shouted, cutting him off, her hands shaking. She wavered on the triggers, and tears fell from her eyes. "God, why can't I hate you?!" She put the guns on the table, and Coop rushed over to her. "Get off of me!" she screamed when he tried to grab her in his arms. She fought against him, but he held her tight.

"I trusted you! You said I was safe with you ... you said I was safe ..." she said through tears that seared into his heart. "What did I ever do to *you*?"

Coop felt his own tears fall. "Nothing. I'm so sorry. You *are* safe, Dev. I'll fix this. I don't know how, but I'll fix this and prove you're safe."

Just then, Coop's attention was caught by the unmistakable sound of his backyard French patio door uncharacteristically sliding open. Alarmed, he whirled around toward to the source of the sound. Devyn looked up as well.

They watched in time to see Grant walking over the threshold and into the living room. Coop had little time to wonder how the patio door he'd always kept locked, unless he was surveilling it, had been unlocked today, as his eyes trained on the intruding man and down to the gun he held at his side.

"Damn, Coop," Grant said in an upbeat tone as he entered the living room, gun now pointed on him. "You're more impressive than I thought. Why, you've managed to find a heart where I swore there wasn't one." His eyes slid to Devyn, and he fixed her with horrible, wild gaze she had never witnessed before. The blood turned to icy slush in her veins and her body stiffened, paralyzed by the dreadful uncertainty of what he planned to do next.

Coop pulled Devyn behind him, and Grant smiled. "Look at this tender moment. ...It's like something out of a horror movie. ...Or, maybe a fairytale, you know, the one with the beast and the beauty. Except, there are two beasts in this version," he quipped.

"Get. Out." Coop retorted, threateningly, hoping the detective would not try to escalate things further.

Grant shrugged. "Fine, as soon as you move out of my way. Devyn, you told me to prove you were a murderer, remember?" He pulled out his phone, and suddenly they were all listening to a recording of what should have been a private conversation between between Devyn and Coop.

"Did you tell him I killed Rayes?"

"No. I know you probably don't believe that, but it's true. I didn't tell him about anything you told me."

"I believe you, which makes this worse. You're going to die for nothing."

He glanced back at Devyn, enjoying the look of horror on her face, savoring it.

"You tapped my phone?!" yelled Coop, incredulous.

Grant pointedly ignored him, focused on the woman behind him. "You really must be crazy about this guy to become so careless. I knew you would show up here once I dropped the hint of his betrayal. You've gone soft, Devyn." His face hardened. "I *know* you killed him. I *always* knew! Now tell me what the *fuck* you did with my brother's body?!"

Devyn moved around Coop and pointed at Grant's stomach. "*You* should know. If I remember correctly, you had four bowls of Rayes at his memorial!"

Grant's eyes widened. "You bitch!" he screamed. "I should have fucking killed you after I killed your sister!"

Devyn felt like the wind had been knocked from her lungs.

Coop could only stare, flabbergasted. "What the *hell* did you say?"

"After Rayes assaulted her I told him to kill her, leave no witnesses. But he wouldn't listen. He'd convinced himself that Bria loved him and wouldn't turn him in. Well, I wasn't about to take any chances," he laughed. "I let the little slut make it to the door before I blew her brains out. But, I'm not letting you get even *that* far."

Grant pulled the trigger and Devyn flinched and shut her eyes.

Feeling Coop's strong arm pull her out of the way, she crashed to the floor. When she looked back at him, Coop had shifted. He had also taken a shot to the arm when he moved to protect her. Blood flowed from his wound.

Silver eyes glowing, the minotaur let out the deepest, most reverberating roar she had ever heard in her life.

"Shit!" Grant shouted as the minotaur shifter charged at him. He raised his gun once more and unloaded the entire clip. Each bullet he fired pierced the minotaur's torso and abdomen, but he relentlessly charged at Grant, anger radiating off of his huge form.

The minotaur's attack was vicious. His sharp, long, horns speared Grant's chest with ease, and the man let out a sharp cry as his impaled form was lifted into the air like a ragdoll. Blood cascaded down his torn shirt and pooled onto the carpet below.

A horrified scream escaped Devyn's throat as she watched the scene unfold. The minotaur swung his head from side to side, and Grant grunted with every motion. With one last, powerful swing of his horns, Grant was thrown several feet across the room. His body hit the wall with a sickening crack, before crumbling to the floor, motionless.

Tearing his gaze away from Grant, Coop locked eyes with Devyn and was met with sheer, unadulterated fear. He attempted to shift to his human form, but was too weak to fully do so, thus, his horns and tail remained. Blood trickled from every wound on his body. As the adrenaline started to wear off, the pain from his injuries quickly set in and began to affect him.

Uneasily, Coop staggered forward.

"Dev —" he said in a broken and pained voice, reaching out as if to comfort her.

Fear and sorrow ravaged Devyn as she watched helplessly as he collapsed to the floor.

"No!" she screamed.

She rushed to his side. With trembling hands, she gathered him into her arms, and desperately shook him in a plea for him to stay awake as his eyes fell closed. "Please ... you're okay. Please." Devyn's tears fell silently onto Coop's cheeks. She did not want to believe she was losing him like this.

This seemed to stir the minotaur shifter. Slowly, he managed to open his eyes enough to focus on her face. A fragile smile tugged at Coop's lips as he raised his hand and tenderly touched her wet cheek.

"I love you," he whispered in a faint voice.

"I love you too," she said in rushed tone. "Just hang in there okay? I'll call the ambulance. You just have to stay awake."

His eyes were already falling shut.

A brilliant light shone from within him in that moment, engulfing his body entirely. "Everything will be okay," he whispered as his eyes closed for the final time.

Before Devyn could even react, the light faded away, and with it, the love of her life.

Chapter 12

One Month Later

"Are you sure you really want to leave?" Trixie asked Devyn as they sat in their favorite restaurant. "I know it's been hard, but we need you."

"I need to do this Trix, I feel like I'm suffocating in this job. This town." Devyn looked at the table behind them and immediately thought of Coop. "Coop gave his life to save mine, and I-I can't process that in a place where everything reminds me of him. With the perpetrators responsible for my sister's death both gone, I feel like Bria is finally at peace," she said, smiling through unshed tears. "Besides, the people still have you. And, you're even scarier than me."

Trixie's bottom lip trembled. "Yeah, right," she said, as her own eyes filled with tears. She wiped the corner of her eyes with her napkin. "I'm really going to miss you, Devyn."

"I'm going to miss you, too. I'm only a phone call and machete away." The two laughed and briefly hugged. "I'll see you later, okay? I love you."

"I love you, too."

Exiting the restaurant, Devyn placed her shades over her eyes and exhaled sharply. She walked over to the nearby lot where she had parked her car. She entered her car and sat inside for a moment with her hand on her key, before glancing up and noticing something on the windshield.

She stepped out of the car and swiped it off the window. Devyn opened the folded flyer when she had reseated herself in the car, only to realize it was an Asterions flyer. Immediately tears formed in her eyes. She bit her lip and willed herself not to cry.

"I always told Vinny I hated that flier. Yellow and red are awful together," a deep voice proclaimed from beside her.

Devyn felt her heart thudding in her chest and spun round to face the source of the sound. Her brain refused to accept what her eyes saw. "You're not real..." she whispered in disbelief.

There sat Cooper in the passenger seat, smiling at her. Glowing, unharmed, and as gorgeous as the day they had first met. He reached up and took off his sunglasses. "I'm real," he reassured her.

Devyn spoke slowly, unsure if she was going crazy. "I saw you die."

He shook his head. "Eh, technically, you saw me disappear to avoid dying," he corrected her. "Take out Grant, send the beacon, and boom, I'm back home to recover."

"Send ... the beacon?" Devyn had no idea what he was talking about.

"Yeah. The beacon," said Coop as if she should know. Quickly realizing they'd never discussed it before, he elaborated. "It's a teleportation signal minotaurs use. Kinda like using a cellphone to call an Uber from a really long distance ... except way more convenient, obviously."

"Ah."

"I told her the lights were over the top, but mother has always had a flair for the dramatic."

"Are you shitting me?!" Devyn shouted, when she had recovered enough from the shock of seeing him. "I really thought you were dead Cooper, and that it was all my fault!"

He cringed at Devyn using his full name. "Why?! I told you that everything would be okay!"

"That's what *everyone* in the movie says when they're dying! How the hell was I supposed to know you meant it?!"

"It's not my fault you didn't believe me. I guess my record isn't spotless, but when we're married, I'll need you to trust me when I tell you things."

"Married?!" she screamed, scaring a passerby. "How the hell do you disappear from the human realm for a month, come back, and think you're just going to claim me as your *wife*?! I swear you are the most arrogant—"

Coop kissed her hard. Pulling away, he seemed to take her breath as well. "You knew that when you met me," he said, grinning. "And you like it, which is why you're going to say 'yes.'" He caressed her face. "I'm sorry it took me so long, but I needed to heal from my wounds and work out some thin — "

Just then, his phone rang, the sound reverberating in the awkward silence between them.

"May I take this?" he asked her with an unfamiliar formality in his tone.

Devyn rolled her eyes at the display. "You didn't need my permission to avoid me for a *whole* month after I thought you died."

Coop answered the call and quickly covered the speaker. "Dev," he whispered quickly. "I wasn't avoiding – Hello?" Someone on the phone had disrupted him. "Right now? Er ... no, no, it's fine. We'll head there now. See you soon."

Coop turned to Devyn who was understandably confused. "There's someone I want you to meet, Devyn. Would you mind heading to my place?"

His question felt loaded with meaning. Devyn's mind raced with questions and possibilities. So much had happened during the last few minutes. *What else could he have in mind?*

"Okay, sure," she said quietly.

He kissed her cheek, "I'll grab my car then," he said and made to leave but she stopped him.

"No, it's fine. I'll drive you."

The car ride was quiet with an underlying sense of uncertainty. They arrived at Coop's house just ten minutes later. Memories, both good and terrible, began rushing back to Devyn as they walked up to Coop's doorway. He opened the door and she followed him inside.

Coop had redecorated since that fateful night when they almost lost their lives - a new carpet, fresh paint and new furniture had replaced any remnants of that night not long ago. Coop took Devyn's jacket and placed it with his in the closet.

"Inside the living room," he spoke quietly, gesturing for her to follow him. Devyn couldn't recall seeing any other cars in the driveway when they had arrived - who could Coop be referring to?

They entered the well-lit living room where a finely dressed, older woman with long dark hair and pale skin, and a tall, handsome younger man with short dark hair and prominent brows sat waiting for them. Devyn noticed both of them had glowing silver eyes. Coop bowed before them, reverently.

"Mother, brother," he spoke softly. "This is my love, Devyn."

"So this is the human you saved," said his mother. It was not a question. Devyn didn't know how to interpret that statement, but when the woman stood and extended her hand with a smile, Devyn accepted it. "It's lovely to meet you. I'm Erinyes. Coop's told us plenty about you. You're just as beautiful as he described."

"T-thank you. And it's nice to meet you too," said Devyn, feeling both flattered and out of her element. Erinyes' aura was captivating and unmistakably powerful, despite her small frame. She looked like she was sweet, but could easily take you out if needed. No wonder Coop was intimidated by her, Devyn thought quietly.

"It's a pleasure, Devyn. I'm Finn," Coop's brother greeted her with an outstretched hand. Devyn shook it as he added. "Coop's completely smitten. You've got him by the horns."

"All right, that's enough now, Finn" Coop laughed, embarrassed, pushing his older brother away from Devyn. Devyn smiled at the flush rising on his cheeks and ears.

When they were all seated together, Coop's mother spoke up. "We came because we wanted to meet the one who had stolen his heart and gave him the strength to finally walk in his purpose."

"What purpose is that?" Devyn asked, turning to Coop.

"I've found a way to honor my role as a young leader of my people, and it's all because of you."

"Me?"

"Yes. See, my father was a politician who brought peace between the Minotaur and Centaur nations, who had been at war for ages. Finn and I were encouraged to follow in his footsteps. But I ran away because I was afraid of not living up to everyone's expectations," he paused, before smiling at her with a confidence she hadn't seen in him before. "But, you've made me realize that I *am* capable. You've risked your life to help those who are forgotten, and you're kind, especially to those who are struggling, myself included. I think that's why I ended up in this town, I needed to meet you. Your bravery and heart inspired me to be better."

Devyn was incredibly touched by his words. "I'm so happy to hear that Coop, and thank you for trusting me enough to share that with me." She recalled her conversation with Vinny, regarding Coop's arranged marriage, and glanced over at his mother who was smiling at them both. "But, is this ok?"

"Us?" Coop clarified, and she nodded. "Of course it is."

He gave his mother a sideways look, as if gauging her opinion and wanting her approval, although even if it didn't come, he wouldn't be deterred.

"Minotaurs have been a very traditional species for centuries, only coupling with our own," started Erinyes in a stern voice as her eyes flitted between her son and Devyn. "Times are changing, however. Originally, I planned an arranged marriage for Cooper," she confessed, unapologetically and quite matter-of-factly. "*But* while he was recovering from his wounds a month ago, Coop let his intentions be known that he only wanted you, Devyn." Erinyes' face softened as she looked at her son. "I saw how much he's changed — how much happier he's become since meeting you. I decided then that I won't stand between you two. Your mutual acceptance of each other is the essence of what Cooper's father taught the Minotaur and Centaur nations: peace begins when we are united in love."

"That's really beautiful," said Devyn. "He's changed me too," she admitted reflectively. "Coop is the most amazing man I've ever met. You've done a wonderful job raising him."

The smile on Erinyes' face was one of genuine acceptance for Devyn, one Devyn gladly returned. When Devyn looked over her shoulder at Coop, he was looking at them both with pure fondness.

Finn flashed his brother a mischievous smile. "Coops," he addressed him. "Bet you fancied yourself a rebel running away from home and your responsibilities like that, but in loving a human, you've become the living *embodiment* of dad's message of unity. It's so poetic, so beautiful it's actually kind of... cringe?"

Coop reached over and punched him playfully in the arm.

"Thank you Finn but shut up please." Finn's goofy nature sometimes made Coop feel like the older brother, but Coop appreciated him all the same.

His brother just laughed before rising to his feet. "Okay guys, you can come out now!"

Just then, Trixie and Vinny walked into the living room, screaming happily. Finn joined them in making noise.

Devyn and Coop looked around and Devyn's eyes doubled in size when she saw her dearest friends. She nearly fell off the couch scrambling to stand up. "What the hell?" she shouted, unable to control herself. "What are you guys doing here?!"

Devyn felt a hand grab her wrist. Coop was softly pulling her back down to her seat next to him.

With her hand still in his, Coop gently kissed her ring finger. "I love you, Devyn," he told her, "and I'm not leaving here without you. I've made that very clear to my family, and I'm making it very clear to *you* now."

Pulling a beautiful white and pink diamond ring from his pocket, he slipped it onto her finger. A tear fell from Devyn's eye, and he wiped it away with his thumb, smiling broadly. "Will you do me the honor of marrying me?"

"I will," she said, smiling. "Arrogance and all."

Coop picked her up and swung her around. Everyone was clapping.

"You've made me very happy," Coop whispered when he put her down.

"I love you," she replied, kissing him. Then, she turned to Trixie and Vinny. "No, really. What're you guys doing here?!"

"Couldn't miss the proposal," said Vinny, beaming.

"You knew about this?!"

Trixie nodded. "Yeah, Coop popped up out of nowhere yesterday and told me to invite you to Asterions. Scared the hell out of me. I almost shot him." The group laughed again. "The plan was to let you go home with Coop, and follow you two back here in time for the proposal. I'm so glad we made it!"

Vinny, who was looking at her fondly, kissed her cheek. "Me too, babe."

"Thanks for not shooting me," said Coop grimacing. "Finn would never let me live down getting shot again."

"It's true," said Finn, grinning, "I'm barely letting him live it down now."

"Shall I teach you some manners?" Trixie said teasingly.

"Don't," warned Coop, "he'd probably like that."

"I would," Finn confirmed cheekily. Trixie gave him a playfully flirtatious look, which he returned good-naturedly before the two broke out in laughter.

Coop rolled his eyes and whispered aloud against Devyn's ear. "Those two have the same chaotic energy." She nodded in agreement, withholding a laugh of her own.

"Hooves off buddy," said Vinny half-jokingly to Finn. He pulled Trixie closer and said, "And haven't you ever heard, 'save a horse, ride a cowboy?'"

"Minotaurs aren't horses, Vin," Trixie deadpanned. "You're thinking of centaurs."

"Geez Vinny," said Finn feigning annoyance. "We don't all look the same."

The silly banter had laughter filling the room, lifting up everyone's spirits higher still. Vinny turned to Devyn, a serious look on his face, "Have the peace you've given others around you, Dev. Be happy. You deserve it."

Trixie nodded beside him. "Yeah Dev, we'll take it from here."

"Thanks you guys," said Devyn, touched.

Trixie walked forward and touched her forearm, giving it a comforting squeeze. "Family looks out for family," she winked. "Just don't forget our invites to the wedding."

Devyn laughed through eyes that brimmed with unshed tears. "You know you'll be the first person I call up, Trix."

Devyn looked around the room at all the wonderful people in her life now. "Thank you, everyone. This really means a lot," she said earnestly. She turned and hugged her fiance. "Thanks, Coop, for always being my safe space."

Leaning down, he clasped her face in his warm, gentle hands. "Forever and always," he said and kissed her deeply.

Author's Note

Thank you for reading Saddled By Desire, the first in my interracial paranormal romance series.

If you enjoyed the story or have encouraging or constructive comments please leave a review! It also helps more readers discover my work, so thank you in advance!

Do you prefer your men, hot, sexy, kind of dangerous and not quite human? Then you'll want to join my email list so you can stay up-to-date on all the latest news about my books, including new releases, sales, and giveaways! Also follow me on Instagram for information on new releases, updates and behind the scenes fun posts.

Let's connect~